Elephant's Ears

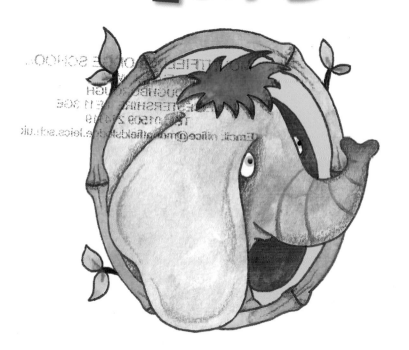

Written by Grace Webster

Illustrated by Emily Golden

Collins

Elephant had gigantic ears that flipped and flopped over his eyes, but he was too scared to visit the ear dressers.

3

Goose tied his ears up with a pink ribbon, but that was too girlie.

5

Chimp made him a hat out of bananas, but that was too sticky.

6

Snail gave him his shell,
but that was too small
and fell off.

So he had to be brave
and visit the ear dressers
with his mummy.

Now he loves the ear dressers and goes there all the time.

Everyone says he has the best ear style of all!

Elephant's ear styles

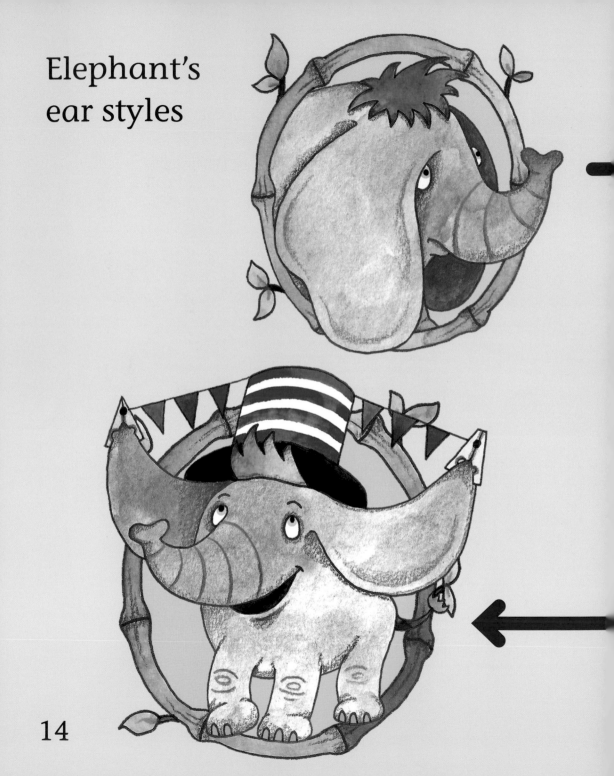

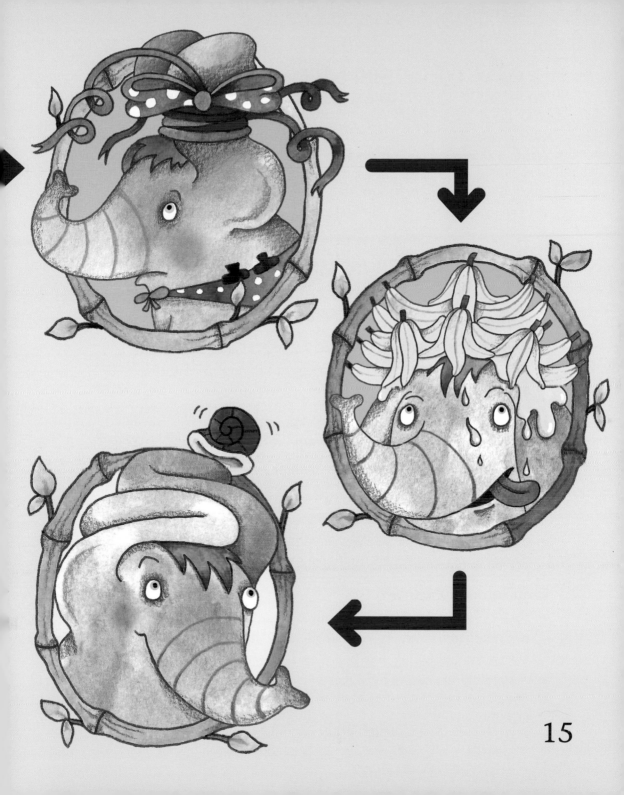

Ideas for reading

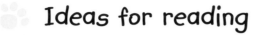

Written by Clare Dowdall, Phd
Lecturer and Primary Literacy Consultant

Learning objectives: read other words of more than one syllable that contain taught GPCs; re-read these books to build up their fluency and confidence in word reading; drawing on what they already know or on background information and vocabulary provided by the teacher; making inferences on the basis of what is being said and done

Curriculum links: Art and Design

High frequency words: had, that, and, over, his, was, he, the, too, with, out, off, so, be, now, there, all

Interest words: elephant, gigantic, enough, ear dressers, goose, girlie, bananas

Resources: whiteboard, interest word cards, paper, pencils, internet, information books about elephants

Word count: 96

Getting started

- Look at the front cover and read the title together. Look at the illustration and ask children what is special about Elephant's ears. Make a list of words that describe his ears and write them on the whiteboard.

- Read the blurb aloud to the children. Discuss what an "ear dresser" might be and what might happen to Elephant at the ear dressers. Encourage children to contribute and listen to each other.

- Introduce the interest words using word cards and help children to decode them.

Reading and responding

- Turn to pp2–3. Read the text together. Dwell on the multisyllabic words *el-e-phant; gi-gan-tic.* Help children to read these longer words, noticing known chunks and syllables.

- Ask children to describe the problem with Elephant's ears. Check that they understand that his ears get in his eyes and stop him seeing. Discuss why elephant might be scared to go to the ear dressers. Support them to use their own examples of places they are nervous to go to, and why.